The Praise for **5Worlds**

A New York Public Library Top Ten Best Books for Kids Selection

A *Publishers Weekly* Best Summer Book

An NPR Great Read of the Year

A Junior Library Guild Selection

"Cinematic beauty."
—*The New York Times Book Review*

"For kids who love fantasy and other-world adventures,
and for any fans of graphic novels, this book is a must-read."
—**R. J. Palacio, #1** *New York Times* **bestselling author of** *Wonder*

★ "Sensitive writing, gorgeous artwork, and riveting plot,
this is a series to keep an eye on."
—*Booklist*, **Starred Review**

★ "A dazzling interplanetary fantasy . . . that will easily appeal
to fans of *Naruto* or *Avatar: The Last Airbender*."
—*Publishers Weekly*, **Starred Review**

"This stellar team has created a gorgeous and entrancing world like no other!"
—**Noelle Stevenson,**
New York Times **bestselling author of** *Nimona*

"Epic action, adventure, and mystery will draw you in, but the heartfelt characters
and their seemingly impossible journey will keep you turning the pages."
—**Lisa Yee, author of the DC Super Hero Girls™ series**

5 Worlds

BOOK 4

THE AMBER ANTHEM

Mark
SIEGEL

Alexis
SIEGEL

Xanthe
BOUMA

Boya
SUN

Matt
ROCKEFELLER

Random House New York

OONA LEE, the young Sand Dancer from Mon Domani

AN TZU, the boy from the slums of Sao Sablo, with **RAM SAM SAM**, a sentient oil being from Salassandra

JAX AMBOY, the superstar Starball player, secretly an android

STAN MOON, head of Stan Moon Industries

THE STORY SO FAR...

To save the **FIVE WORLDS** from dying out, **OONA** and her friends must light all five ancient beacons: white, red, blue, yellow, and green.

For centuries, **the Living Fire** that lights beacons was the stuff of legend—until three children produced it on the blue world of **Toki**.

The destinies of **OONA, AN TZU,** and **JAX** collided in the wreckage of Chrysalis Stadium as war raged on **Mon Domani**.

With help from her friends, clumsy **OONA** summoned a **Sand Warrior** and lit the **White Beacon** of Mon Domani.

On Toki, **OONA** fought against an evil prince and discovered the truth of her heritage—that she was born on the blue planet.

The battle against the **Cobalt Prince**, and the evil **MIMIC** controlling him, was won, but at great cost: **OONA**'s sister **JESSA** sacrificed herself.

On **Salassandra, JAX** merged with a Salassi spirit known as a **DEVOTI** to become human.

AN TZU suffers from a mysterious **Vanishing Illness** and is beginning to fade away. He uses prosthetics to help maintain his physical form.

On **Moon Yatta, OONA** trained with **MASTER ZELLE**, who taught her how to create **portals** to defeat the **Red Maze**.

Using a portal, **OONA** lit the **Red Beacon.** Immediately afterward, **VECTOR SANDERSON**, now the new Prince of Toki, lit the **Blue Beacon.**

STAN MOON, possessed by the evil **MIMIC**, was elected head of Moon Yatta. He has vowed to hunt down **OONA** and her friends.

OONA, JAX, and **AN TZU** are now traveling aboard the **Flitori**, heading toward Salassandra and the **Yellow Beacon....**

I see moonbeams in your smile!
I hear sunbeams in your voice!
I see starlight in your eyes!
    —CASCADELLE, "THE TOKI GIRL FROM MON DOMANI"

I WAS LOOKING AT THE SUN AND SAW *THE FELID GODS...* FROM LONG AGO...

BUT WHY? WHAT HAVE THEY GOT TO DO WITH YOU?

I DON'T KNOW!

WHAT DID YOU MEAN, "HOME"? THAT'S A *SUN.*

HOW CAN HOME BE ON A SUN?

NOT *ON* A SUN. *IN A* SUN!

THE *COBALT PRINCE* SAID THE SUN ISN'T HOW WE THINK. RIGHT HERE, *INSIDE* THE FIERY BALL, IS A COOL WORLD!

THE TOKI PRINCE? WASN'T HE *LYING* HALF THE TIME?

I BELIEVE *THAT PART* WAS TRUE.

CHAPTER 1
THE GOLDEN GLYPHS

OONA!

WAKE UP! WE'RE HERE!

WHOA. THAT'S NOT AN OLD-FUEL!

HOW COME *THEY* GET TO FLY WHEN ALL OF OUR *RED-GRIDS* ARE GROUNDED?

I'VE SEEN THAT SHIP. SOME KIND OF *ORGANIC* TECH. BELONGS TO THE THREE *MAD CAPTAINS.* YOU KNOW WHO'S ON BOARD THAT?

WHO?

THAT *SAND DANCER GIRL.* THE ONE WHO'S GOING AROUND LIGHTING THE OLD *BEACONS* AND WRECKING EVERYTHING.

THERE! GET US CLOSE TO THE GREAT PYRAMID!

12

THE *BIG PEOPLE* SEEM LIKE THEY ARE SLEEPWALKING.

THE SLUMBERING *KYOJIN* ARE IN A KIND OF *TRANCE.* THEY CARRY SLOW CARGO AROUND FOR MONEY AND RARELY SPEAK. THOUGH EVER SINCE *THE WHITE BEACON* TURNED ON, THEY'VE BEEN HUMMING A LITTLE *MUSIC.*

THOK!

THUNK!

THOSE CHILDREN ARE THROWING STONES AT IT.

HEY! STOP DOING THAT!!

YOUR **VANISHING ILLNESS** IS GETTING WORSE!

JAX, WHAT CAN WE DO?

WE'LL NEED TO FIND YOU MORE PROSTHETICS, OR AT LEAST SPARE PARTS.

AT THE RATE IT'S SPREADING, I'LL NEED SPARE PARTS EVERYWHERE.

...

EVERY DAY YOU'RE GETTING MORE *HUMAN,* JAX, AND I'M GETTING TO BE MORE *ROBOT!*

THAT POSTER!

ARE YOU
OONA LEE?

I AM.

20

THE BEACON! IT'S...

...ENCASED IN A KIND OF **INDESTRUCTIBLE AMBER.** IT'S ALWAYS BEEN THIS WAY. SINCE THE AGE OF THE **FELID GODS.**

OONA, GO AHEAD AND LIGHT IT.

RRR!!

LET'S DANCE, *RAM SAM SAM!*

RRM SM!!

IT'S HER.

SHE'S ABOUT TO LIGHT OUR BEACON.

SHOULD WE SOUND AN ALERT?

ARE YOU *CRAZY?* ISN'T *SHE* WHAT WE'RE ALL WAITING FOR?!

WAIT, LOOK!

SHE SHOULD GO BACK WHERE SHE CAME FROM!

foof!!

THE LIVING FIRE!!

BY THE GREAT QUEEN! SO IT'S TRUE?

SHOULD THE AMBER MELT AWAY...?

IF SO, IT'S NOT WORKING.

THAT'S ALL I CAN DO.

MISS LEE, WE SCHOLARS AREN'T SURE WHAT TO EXPECT IF YOU LIGHT IT.

YES, WHAT WILL HAPPEN? *WHY* ARE YOU DOING ALL THIS?

YOU KNOW THE WORLDS ARE OVERHEATING.

LIGHTING THE BEACONS IS THE ONLY WAY TO BRING THEM BACK INTO BALANCE.

BALANCE? AFTER THE *RED BEACON* WAS LIT, THE *CLEAN SHIPS* STOPPED RUNNING. YOU CALL THAT *BALANCE?*

I HEAR THE FIVE WORLDS HAVE EVEN STARTED *MOVING APART!*

MON DOMANI WAS PARCHED WITH *DROUGHT* BEFORE I LIT ITS BEACON...THEN *RAIN* CAME TO THE MOTHER WORLD.

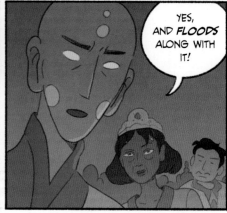

YES, AND *FLOODS* ALONG WITH IT!

BALANCE WILL COME WHEN *ALL BEACONS* ARE LIT! THE *FELID GODS* BUILT *FIVE*...

AND ONLY *THREE* BEACONS ARE LIT!

BUT BASICALLY, YOU'RE NOT SURE *WHAT* LIGHTING THE BEACON WILL DO TO US HERE ON *SALASSANDRA*.

ARE YOU?

LOOK! UP THERE!

SOME KIND OF WRITING?

WHAT DOES THAT SAY?

HM.

DO ANY OF YOU KNOW WHAT THAT SAYS?

HM.

HOW CURIOUS.

FASCINATING.

IT'S THE *ANCIENT LANGUAGE!* I CAN'T TRANSLATE IT--THAT PART OF MY *UNCLE JEP'S ARCHIVE* IS DAMAGED. DO YOU THINK ANYONE CAN?

I KNOW SOMEONE WHO MIGHT.

VECTOR SANDERSON.

HOW DARE YOU APPROACH OUR SACRED BEACON?!

MAKE WAY FOR URMUTH, THE PROTECTOR OF ALL FAITHS!

RRR...

STOMP STOMP!

URMUTH!

HIM AGAIN?! DIDN'T WE RUN HIM OUT OF TOWN?!*

STOP THEM!

ARREST THEM!

* SEE 5W2: *THE COBALT PRINCE*

30

HEY!

CLIMB UP, AN TZU.

SHF

FWA AAH

FIPSSSH!

DEAR CITIZEN FEEDERS!

JOIN ME LIVE FROM *AMBRINE* FOR THE *HEROIC* ARREST OF A MEMBER OF THE *TERRORIST* CELL KNOWN AS *THE ORDER OF THE QUEEN'S ARM!*

THANK YOU SO MUCH FOR TAKING THE TIME TO BE WITH US TODAY, *LORD URMUTH.*

GOOD TO BE HERE, *PEET.*

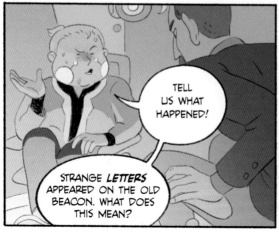

TELL US WHAT HAPPENED!

STRANGE *LETTERS* APPEARED ON THE OLD BEACON. WHAT DOES THIS MEAN?

OH, IT'S PERFECTLY CLEAR.

THAT'S AN ANCIENT MESSAGE WARNING US ABOUT *INFIDELS DEFILING OUR SACRED BEACON.*

SOURCES SAY THAT WAS THE NOTORIOUS *OONA LEE.* STIRRING UP TROUBLE IN *EVERY* WORLD, ISN'T SHE?

SHOULD WE BE *SCARED?*

OR *TERRIFIED?*

REMAIN ON HIGH ALERT! YOU HAVE TO PROTECT YOUR BEACON!

HIGH ALERT INDEED! AS YOU KNOW, LIGHTING THE RED BEACON WAS A *DISASTER* FOR *MOON YATTA'S* ECONOMY.

EXACTLY. IT TOOK OUT *THE TRANSPORT GRID!*

AND *THAT* MEANS NO MORE CLEAN SHIPS FOR ANY OF THE WORLDS, DOESN'T IT? IS THAT CAUSE FOR *OUTRAGE?* OR FOR JUST PLAIN *RAGE?*

THE *FLITORI* SHOULD BE ACROSS THERE...

THE *POLICE* ARE TAKING IT! IT'S NOT SAFE NOW! DON'T LET THEM SEE YOU.

WHAT IS THIS *UNREGISTERED* TECHNOLOGY, ANYWAY? HOW IS IT EVEN FLYING WITHOUT *OLD FUEL?*

IT'S *ORGANIC!* FROM *GRIMBO-E.* THE SHIP WAS A GIFT TO US!

I ASSURE YOU IT MEETS EVERY SAFETY CODE--

CLUNK

CLNK!

WHERE'S O'ZIRG?

THEY *ARRESTED* HIM!

OH NO.

AND THE *FLITORI* IS IN CHAINS?! WHAT WILL THEY DO TO IT?

LEAVE THE *FLITORI* TO US, *OONA!* YOU GO LIGHT *THE YELLOW BEACON!*

I HAVE TO TALK TO *VECTOR SANDERSON* ON *TOKI!*

WHERE CAN I GET AN *INTERWORLD LINK?*

GET TO THE *GREENS MARKET!* THE PLANT PEOPLE WON'T TURN YOU IN. THERE'S AN INTERWORLD CAFÉ CALLED *THE SUCCULENTS INN.*

SHOW THIS *BADGE.*

NOW *GO!*

I MUST GET BACK OR THEY'LL BE SUSPICIOUS.

EASY WITH THOSE *TUGSHIPS!* YOU'LL ANSWER FOR ANY DAMAGE!

STAN MOON! THERE'S NO GETTING AWAY FROM HIM, IS THERE?

DON'T YOU UNDERSTAND *ANYTHING*, URMUTH? *TELL THEM SHE DIDN'T.* AND THEN THE DAY *AFTER THAT...*

TELL THEM *SHE REALLY DID!* AND *HOW DARE SHE?*

BUT... WHICH IS IT...?

EXACTLY.

ONCE PEOPLE CAN'T TELL *WHAT IS TRUE,* OR DON'T BELIEVE *ANYTHING IS TRUE* ANYMORE--

THEY'RE *YOURS* TO DO WITH AS YOU PLEASE.

BUT ON THAT INTERVIEW *I JUST SAID* THAT--

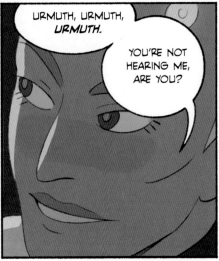

URMUTH, URMUTH, *URMUTH.*

YOU'RE NOT HEARING ME, ARE YOU?

THE *GREENS MARKET* DIDN'T USED TO LOOK LIKE THIS.

SOME OF THE PLANT PEOPLE DON'T LOOK SO WELL.

LIKE ON *MON DOMANI.* THEY'RE LEFT BEHIND.

BUT *AMBRINE* IS A RICH CITY! PLANT PEOPLE CAN'T BE LACKING *WATER* HERE...!

SURE THEY CAN.

IF *STAN MOON* OWNS THE NATURAL SPRINGS.

MOM! ORDER OF THE QUEEN'S ARM!

WELCOME. YES, WE KNOW WHO YOU ARE.

EXCUSE ME, DO YOU KNOW WHAT THIS IS?

FLOWER, SHOW THEM UPSTAIRS.

50

I'D LOVE TO DANCE, *RAM SAM SAM.* BUT WE HAVE TO REACH *VECTOR* NOW.

MOON *TOKI*

OFF-WORLD CALL FOR YOU, *PRINCE VECTOR.*

NOT NOW, *THORN!* THE FORMER COUNCIL MEMBERS KEEP STIRRING UP TROUBLE--

IT'S FROM *OONA LEE!*

BIP BP

FREE TOKI

WHERE IS OUR PRINCE

OONA?!

YES, I'LL TAKE IT.

51

VECTOR...HOW'S LIFE AS A *TOKI ROYAL?*

ACK! THINGS ARE BAD FOR *MOST* PEOPLE HERE. I SIT ON THE THRONE, BUT I CAN'T SEEM TO MAKE THINGS *BETTER.*

WAIT, BUT... *YOU LIT THE BEACON!* THAT *HELPED* TOKI, RIGHT?

THE BLUE BEACON HAS STIRRED UP A THIRST FOR *JUSTICE.* EVERYONE KNOWS IT'S TIME FOR *CHANGE.*

BUT THE FORMER *HIGH COUNCIL* IS *FIGHTING CHANGE* AND INTERFERING WITH MY REFORMS!

I TRIED TO APPEAL TO THEIR *DECENCY,* BUT IT'S NOT WORKING.

DECENCY?!

THEY HAVE NO DECENCY! DO THEY SHOW HIM ANY DECENCY?

DO THEY EVEN CARE ABOUT THE *ASSASSINATION ATTEMPTS* ON VECTOR? THEY'RE *CRIMINALS,* WORTHLESS--

THANKS, *MAGDA,* BUT I WAS KIND OF HOPING FOR A PRIVATE CONVERSATION...?

ASSASSINATION ATTEMPTS?! VECTOR?? YOUR EAR!!

CLOSE CALL. BUT I'M FINE.

VECTOR! BUT WHO...?!

SOME PEOPLE FEEL *BUSINESS WAS BETTER UNDER THE MIMIC'S RULE....* UNTIL ALL THE BEACONS ARE LIT, WE SHOULD EXPECT A FIGHT FROM *THOSE WHO PROFIT FROM DARKNESS.*

HOW'S THAT GOLD BEACON?

TO LIGHT *THIS ONE,* I NEED YOUR HELP DECODING SOME *OLD GLYPHS!*

REMEMBER THE SAND CASTLE MUSEUM?*

THE DAY I CRASHED INTO YOU?

YOU THINK I'D EVER FORGET?

CAN YOU READ THIS?

IT'S THE OLD *FELID* RUNNING SCRIPT...

LET'S SEE... ONE...TEN...

AH! *YES!*

* SEE 5W1: *THE SAND WARRIOR*

53

STRANGE DREAMS

HOW ARE YOU GONNA LIGHT THE *BEACON*?

WILL IT BLOW OUT ALL THE MACHINES, LIKE ON *MOON YATTA*?

THAT MUST'VE BEEN *BLOOMING!!*

I HAVE, LIKE, *A ZILLION* QUESTIONS FOR YOU GUYS...

THANKS, *FLOWER,* MAYBE TOMORROW... WE'VE HAD A REALLY LONG DAY.

OH, OKAY, OKAY, DON'T MIND ME.

BUT YOU CAN TOTALLY COUNT ON ME TO KEEP A *SECRET,* TOO!

I'M QUIET AS A *CREEPING MOSS.*

I WANT TO HELP. I CAN HELP.

YES, THANKS FOR EVERYTHING, *FLOWER.* GOOD NIGHT!

PHEW! SHE'S A BIT MUCH....

HER FAMILY IS A GREAT HELP.

I HOPE WE'RE SAFE HERE.

THINGS HAVEN'T WORKED OUT TOO WELL TODAY.

AT LEAST WE KNOW WHAT THE *GLYPHS* SAY.

YEAH. WE HAVE TO FIND THE *AMBER ANTHEM.*

AND GET *TEN THOUSAND* PEOPLE TO SING IT WITH US.

AND ALONG THE WAY, FREE *O'ZIRG* FROM PRISON!

AND AVOID *URMUTH'S GOONS,* WHO WANT TO JAIL *US* TOO.

WE'VE SEEN WORSE, *OONA.*

WE'LL DO IT TOGETHER.

THANKS, GUYS. ⟨*YAWN*⟩

GOOD NIGHT, *OONA.*

GIVE ME YOUR LEG, AN TZU.

WE ASK **EVERYONE WE CAN** ABOUT THE ANTHEM.

AND GATHER A HUGE CROWD TO SING IT.

RIGHT!

SO...THAT'S THE PLAN.

THAT'S IT?

YUP.

ON **SALASSANDRA**, YOU CAN'T GET **THREE** RELIGIOUS PEOPLE TO AGREE ABOUT ANYTHING, LET ALONE **TEN THOUSAND**...!

JAX, DO YOU SUPPOSE YOU HAVE *THAT MANY* STARBALL FANS?

I COULD PROBABLY FIND *TEN TIMES* THAT!

BUT WE DON'T HAVE A *SONG* FOR THEM TO SING.

I'LL RETURN TO THE *PYRAMID.* THERE ARE *SCHOLARS* THERE.

SOMEONE WILL KNOW ABOUT THIS *ANTHEM.*

OR POINT ME IN THE RIGHT DIRECTION.

BUT HOW? *URMUTH'S* POLICE ARE TRYING TO ARREST US!

WE CAN BARELY GET AROUND THE CITY...

I NEED A DIFFERENT LOOK. *JAX...* CAN YOU *CUT HAIR?*

A *CHANGE OF CLOTHES* WOULD HELP YOU BLEND IN, TOO.

WHAT, YOU'VE BEEN *SPYING* ON US?

HOW LONG HAVE *YOU* BEEN UP THERE?

UM... YOU'RE IN *MY* BEDROOM.

HERE. THIS WON'T SCREAM *"MOON YATTA TOURIST"* SO MUCH.

THANK YOU, *FLOWER. AN TZU,* YOU SHOULDN'T GO WANDERING TOO FAR.

I'LL TAKE CARE OF HIM! AND I CAN HELP!

UGH, WE DON'T *NEED* HELP.

HUH!

WE'LL ASK *PLANT PEOPLE* ABOUT THE *ANTHEM,* TOO.

AND YOU, *RAM SAM SAM*, YOU SPLIT INTO *THREE PARTS* AGAIN, OKAY? SO WE CAN STAY IN TOUCH?

RRM

SM

SMM

NOT BAD.

ADD THIS *PILGRIM PETAL MASK,* AND YOU SHOULD BE ABLE TO WALK DOWN A STREET WITHOUT GETTING ARRESTED.

SEE? I'M HELPFUL.

WELL? HAVE YOU FOUND THEM YET?

MEANWHILE, AT **STAN MOON'S** PRIVATE AIRFIELD

UM...

IT'S HARD TO GET ANY COOPERATION FROM THE **PLANT CREATURES.** THEY'RE VERY STUBBORN....

I NEED SOMEONE I CAN **TRULY** COUNT ON.

BUT, SIR....

GOOD THING I BROUGHT JUST SUCH A **PERSON** WITH ME.

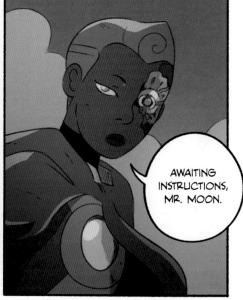

AWAITING INSTRUCTIONS, MR. MOON.

Chapter 5

THE AVIARY

THANK YOU! THANK YOU! SO GOOD TO BE BACK HERE!

ARE THE *LEATHERHEADS* BACK TOGETHER?

NO...AS YOU KNOW, I'VE BEEN TRAVELING WITH *OONA LEE, THE LIGHTER OF BEACONS!*

THAT'S RIGHT! SHE'S HERE ON *SALASSANDRA* RIGHT NOW!

WHEN'S YOUR NEXT GAME?

RIGHT NOW, I'M FOCUSED ON LIGHTING THE--

YOU TOOK A *BEATING* ON *YATTA!* WHAT HAPPENED?

WAIT.

STOP.

YOU DO UNDERSTAND IF WE *DON'T* LIGHT THE BEACONS, THE WORLDS WILL *OVERHEAT?*

ALL THE WORLDS.

IF THE WORLD'S KEEP OVERHEATING, THERE WILL BE NO MORE STARBALL!

NO STARBALL?!

OH NO!!

THAT'S RIGHT, NO STARBALL!

WE CAN'T HAVE THAT!

COME BACK TONIGHT AT SECOND SUNSET! AND BRING ALL YOUR FRIENDS!

BRING EVERYONE YOU KNOW. WE NEED YOUR HELP TO SAVE THE FIVE WORLDS! SEE YOU TONIGHT!

MEANWHILE...

YOU NEW, TOO? I JUST JOINED THE *CATMOONDU PILGRIMS!*

OH...?

THEY'RE HEARING ALL SORTS OF *UNKIND THINGS* ABOUT YOU.

FROM THAT *PEET BOWL* ON THE *CITIZEN FEEDS.*

WHEREVER THERE IS IGNORANCE, THERE IS ALWAYS A *PEET BOWL* FEEDING ON IT. BUT WHERE THERE IS THE *LIVING FIRE, THINGS ARE SHOWN FOR WHAT THEY REALLY ARE.*

IT'S BEAUTIFUL...

MY WINGED FRIENDS TELL ME SO MUCH.

THE *SAPPHIRE SPARROW* IS TRILLING ITS *HIGH ALERT.* IT SENSES DANGER, A CHANGE IN THE BALANCE OF OUR WORLD.

THE PAIR OF GREAT *PTUHULI BIRDS* USUALLY KEEP TO THEMSELVES.

BUT THEY HUDDLED WITH THE *RUBY BARBET,* WITH WHOM THEY NORMALLY *QUARREL.* THE WHOLE *AVIARY* IS BUZZING...

...IN ANTICIPATION OF *IMPORTANT EVENTS,* BUT FEARFUL OF HOW THEY WILL TURN OUT.

HOW...?!

THAT'S WHAT MY FELLOW SCHOLARS ASKED--HOW COULD THE **BLIND SAND DANCER** TEND TO THE AVIARY?

KRI KRI

BUT YOU HAVE A SECRET...

HA! A SECRET HIDDEN IN PLAIN SIGHT...

THAT WE ARE ALL CONNECTED TO WHAT SURROUNDS US...AND ONLY **THINK** WE ARE SEPARATE AND ISOLATED.

SO IT'S A FEELING?

A **KNOWING FEELING.** THE SAND OF SALASSANDRA RESPONDS TO **BELIEF.**

SEEMS LIKE THERE'S PLENTY OF THAT ON SALASSANDRA. PEOPLE HERE BELIEVE *ALL KINDS* OF THINGS.

MOST OF THAT IS *BLIND FAITH.*

WISHFUL THINKING OF THE DESPERATE... EXPLOITED BY THE UNSCRUPULOUS.

BELIEF IS BORN OF KNOWLEDGE THAT YOU'VE JOINED WITH THE *WHOLE* OF YOURSELF. IT'S LIKE THE *LIVING FIRE*--IT CAN'T BE *FAKED.*

SHE IS REAL. SHE IS WHAT WE'VE ALL BEEN GUARDING THE BEACON FOR.

WHAT DOES SHE *NEED?*

I NEED TO LEARN THE *ANCIENT AMBER ANTHEM!* WHO KNOWS IT?

WHAT ABOUT THE *SINGING WEAVERS?* HAS SHE ASKED THEM?

HM. NOT A BAD IDEA. THEY MOVE AROUND, THOUGH. THEY COULD BE ANYWHERE.

I SAW THEM AT *GOLDEN GROVE* LAST. I COULD TAKE HER THERE.

THANK YOU. I'LL TAKE YOU UP ON THAT.

THERE IS A QUESTION THAT TROUBLES ME, THOUGH. **WHO ELSE** DID THE GODS ENDOW WITH THE **LIVING FIRE**?

UM, WELL, THERE WERE THREE OF US.

MY SISTER, **JESSA**.

A BOY CALLED **VECTOR**. HE'S THE NEW **TOKI** PRINCE NOW.

AND... WELL, ME.

WHY WOULD THE GREAT GODS GRANT THE LIVING FIRE TO **THREE TOKI CHILDREN**? AND NO ONE ELSE?

YES, GOOD QUESTION. WHY?

HOW ABOUT WE DISCUSS THAT WHEN **MISS OONA** IS DONE LIGHTING THE BEACON?

Chapter 6

THE SINGING WEAVERS

THE *WEAVERS?* NO, THEY'RE NOT ALLOWED IN OUR *SAFFRON SANCTUARY.*

DON'T YOU KNOW *WE* HAVE *THE REAL BEACON?* THAT BIG ONE IN *AMBRINE* IS A FAKE!

SPLRRR

YOU CAN ASK *THE GOLD KEEPERS* ON THAT HILL...

BUT YOU'RE *WASTING YOUR TIME* LOOKING FOR THAT *AMBER ANTHEM*-- ALL YOU NEED IS TO CHANT OUR *GOLD INVOCATION*...

RRR

RSS!

RS!

OH, LOOK! OTHER DROPS OF *LIVING OIL?*

LIKE YOU? ARE THERE MORE OF YOU, *RAM SAM SAM?*

THEY SAY WE SHOULD FIND *THE SINGING WEAVERS* IN THE NEXT TOWN.

BUT THEY ASKED IF YOU'D BE WILLING TO LEAD THEM IN A SIMPLE SAND DANCE.

SAID THEY'D BE *HONORED.*

WE DON'T NEED ANY DELIVERIES HERE!

GO ON, SHOO!

WHAT'S THAT *BEAST* DOING THERE *GAWKING?*

WAIT A SECOND! HE DIDN'T DO ANYTHING TO YOU!

UM, SIR? DID YOU LIKE THE DANCING?

IT'S POINTLESS, OONA. IT DOESN'T UNDERSTAND YOU.

GO!

SCRAM!

SHOO!

I SEE MOONBEAMS IN YOUR SMILE! I HEAR SUNBEAMS IN YOUR VOICE!

THEY LIKE MUSIC. *CASCADELLE* BEST OF ALL.

I SEE STARLIGHT IN YOUR EYES!

THIS TREATMENT CAN'T BE RIGHT.

EXCUSE ME, I WAS HOPING TO FIND THE *SINGING WEAVERS.* THIS MUSIC...

YES, PLAYING ONE OF THEIR SONGS. TIDYING UP FOR THEIR RETURN.

CAN I HELP YOU WITH ANYTHING?

OONA HERE IS THE LIGHTER OF BEACONS...

LIGHTER OF BEACONS!! THE WEAVERS WILL BE THRILLED! TO TELL THE TRUTH, THEY SHOULD'VE BEEN BACK YESTERDAY...

DID THEY GO FAR?

INTO THE NEARBY MOUNTAINS. HAD TO CHECK THE *PROTECTIVE LATTICE* AROUND *SULFUR SWAMP*... REPORTS OF A DISTURBANCE...

SULFUR SWAMP?! OH NO!

WHY? WHAT'S *SULFUR SWAMP?*

WHAT'S LEFT OF THE **ANCIENT LEADERS** WHO STAYED LOYAL TO THE **TRAITOR**--THE ONE WHO BETRAYED THE GREAT **QUEEN**...

DON'T GO NEAR THEM, **OONA**! THOSE WHO DO NEVER COME BACK.

I HAVE TO HELP. LEAD ME TO YOUR FRIENDS!

THOSE PEOPLE WEREN'T THE LIGHTER OF BEACONS.

SO YOU **WEAVERS** HAVE BEEN KEEPING THOSE **WRAITHS** LOCKED UP UNTIL NOW?

YES, WE SANG **POWER** INTO A ROPE FENCE, AND THEY'VE NEVER BEEN ABLE TO GET PAST IT BEFORE.

SO WHAT'S CHANGED?

HEAR FOR YOURSELF...

SULFUR SWAMP

THE GREAT ONE HAS RETURNED!

THE GREAT ONE HAS RETURNED!

GREAT ONE!

YES, ALMOST THERE...

STOMP—

STOMP! STOMP!

I ALWAYS KNEW *OONA LEE* WOULD NEVER AMOUNT TO MUCH.... NOT UP TO THE TASK, IS SHE, PLUMB?

SHE'S A *HUGE DISAPPOINTMENT.* COULDN'T FILL HER *SISTER'S* SHOES...

DEAN PLUMB?! BUT HOW...?

EVEN *MASTER ZELLE* COULDN'T TEACH HER MUCH!

JESSA?!

NO WONDER HER JOURNEY ENDS IN A SWAMP.

NO! NO!

SHLP

TIME TO STOP FIGHTING, *OONA.* ACCEPT THAT YOU'RE PART OF A *STRONGER POWER* NOW.

THE ONE THING...

I'M SORRY, I JUST COULDN'T BEAT THOSE WRAITHS. TOO MANY...TOO POWERFUL...

YOU BRING THE GREATEST OF GIFTS...

...LIGHTER OF BEACONS.

THE LIVING FIRE!

THE LIVING FIRE CAN BE... TRANSFERRED?!

THE *TRAITOR* WHO TURNED ON HIS *QUEEN!*

YOU'RE NOT THE *FIRST* PERSON TO ASK US ABOUT *THE AMBER ANTHEM*....

YOU'LL NEVER GUESS WHO IT WAS, YEARS AGO....

CASCADELLE HERSELF!

SHE SPENT YEARS COLLECTING ALL THE *FOLKLORE* SHE COULD.

BUT WE COULDN'T HELP HER WITH THAT AMBER ANTHEM.

MAYBE SHE'S HAD BETTER LUCK SINCE.

YOU SHOULD SEEK *HER* OUT.

DO YOU HAVE ANY IDEA WHERE SHE IS NOW?

NO. SHE RETIRED, AFTER HER *FAREWELL TOUR.*

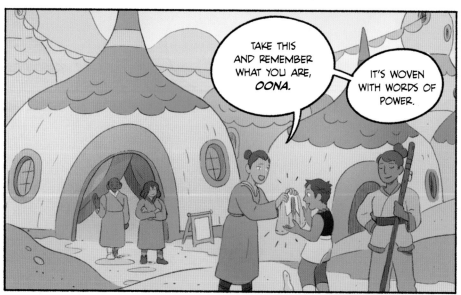

TAKE THIS AND REMEMBER WHAT YOU ARE, *OONA.*

IT'S WOVEN WITH WORDS OF POWER.

WE NEED TO FIND *CASCADELLE....*

SOMEONE IN *AMBRINE* WILL KNOW WHERE SHE IS. SHE HAS SO MANY FANS.

LIKE THE *KYOJIN* PEOPLE.

YES, THOSE *BEASTS* REALLY LIKE HER MUSIC, TOO.

BUT THEY AREN'T "*BEASTS*"! THEY'RE CHILDREN OF THE GREAT QUEEN, LIKE YOU AND ME!

HONESTLY, *OONA*, YOU'VE BEEN ON *SALASSANDRA* FOR, WHAT, THREE DAYS? HOW CAN YOU--

I JUST *KNOW,* WITH EVERY PART OF ME, THAT--

WAIT...I *BELIEVE!* WHAT WAS IT THE WISE SAND DANCER SAID AT THE AVIARY? *THE SAND OF SALASSANDRA RESPONDS TO BELIEF!*

UM, *OONA?* IS EVERYTHING ALL RIGHT?

YES! AND I THINK I CAN OFFER YOU A *SHORTCUT* BACK TO THE OLD BEACON!

I'M **JORTH**, BY THE WAY.

HI, **JORTH!**

CL-AP!

UM, THIS DOESN'T SEEM LIKE A GREAT IDEA.... THIS KID IS A STRANGER....

MY FRIEND'S A **HALF-SAP LIKE US, AN TZU.** I'M SURE YOU'LL LIKE HIM!

LOOK, WE **HAVE** A LEAD, SO MAYBE NOT THIS TIME....

IT'S OKAY. I GET IT.

WE HAVE **TOO MUCH** SAP FOR THE FULL-BLOODS AND **NEVER ENOUGH** FOR THE **FULL VEGETALS** TO TRUST US.

I'M USED TO IT. IT'S FINE....

NO, YOU KNOW WHAT? YOU'RE RIGHT.

LET'S DO THIS!

LET'S GO!

WOW! SEEING THOSE *SHAPESHIFTERS* MUST'VE BEEN SOMETHING ELSE!

YEAH, IT SURE WAS....

IS IT MUCH FURTHER?

WE'RE ALMOST THERE...JUST THIS WAY...

I'M SORRY, AN TZU.

I HAD NO CHOICE.

SORRY? SORRY FOR WHAT?

THEY HAVE MY *FAMILY.* THIS WAS THE ONLY WAY TO *FREE* THEM....

111

HEY, WHAT DO YOU THINK YOU'RE DOING? THAT'S MY STUFF!

MOST DEPRESSING CHILDREN'S BOOK EVER...

STAY OUT OF MY THINGS!

GRAB!

EASY, *HALF-SAP!* I JUST SAVED YOUR LIFE!

YOU'RE WELCOME!

WHAT'S THAT, *RAM SAM SAM?*

JAX IS NEARBY AND COMING HERE? GOOD!

BUT WAIT! ISN'T THAT HIM? *HEY, JAX! OVER HERE!*

JAX?!

I COULD'VE *SWORN* I JUST *SAW YOU* DISAPPEAR INTO THAT BUILDING!

WHAT, THAT ONE?

ZW-ING

KSH PSYDO

OONA, TAKE COVER!

?!

JUMP

SLAM!!

SO YOU THINK YOU'RE *SPECIAL?* BETTER THAN US? I'LL TEACH YOU, YOU JUMPED-UP *J.A.X. MODEL!*

THUMP!

PYOO!

OH! I NEED *THAT* UPGRADE! COULD COME IN *HANDY!*

ZAP!

JUMP!

TMP!

SUCCULENTS INN

A LITTLE LATER

WHAT?! STAN MOON HAS A *FAKE JAX*? AND HE'S TRYING TO *KILL OONA*?!

NEITHER OF YOU IS SAFE. *AN TZU, FLOWER* TOLD US ABOUT YOUR CLOSE CALL WITH *STAN MOON.*

YOU HAVE TO STAY HERE, UNDER THE PROTECTION OF THE PLANT PEOPLE.

I KNOW YOU WANT TO BE OF USE, *AN TZU,* BUT RIGHT NOW WE CAN'T RISK *STAN MOON* ATTACKING YOU AGAIN.

I CAN'T JUST SIT HERE WHILE YOU'RE RISKING YOUR LIFE!

I WILL ACCOMPANY *OONA* WHEREVER SHE NEEDS TO GO, FROM NOW ON...

UNTIL I MANAGE TO STOP THAT *KILLER ANDROID*...WHO LOOKS JUST LIKE *ME.*

AND YOU NEED TO REST, *AN TZU.* *DON'T GO OUT BY YOURSELF.*

FINE.

HEY, *AN TZU*, WE'RE BACK!

AN TZU?

AN TZU?

RAM SAM SAM, CAN YOU SHOW US WHERE HE IS?

.RMM

SSM!

OH NO, HE'S IN DANGER!

135

MR. MOON!!

ARE YOU NO USE FOR ANYTHING? HOW COULD YOU NOT CATCH THE *SAND DANCER* AND THE *STARBALL PLAYER?*

DO I HAVE TO DO *EVERYTHING* MYSELF?

I'M SO SORRY, *MR. MOON!* THE *POLICE...* MISTOOK YOUR INSTRUCTIONS--

YOU PATHETIC *DOLT!* YOU CAN'T RUB TWO BRAIN CELLS TOGETHER BUT WANT TO BE A LEADER!

PLEASE, *MR. MOON,* GIVE ME ANOTHER CHANCE! I WON'T DISAPPOINT YOU AGAIN.

140

142

IS THIS WHAT IT HAS COME TO?

SOME PUNY SAND DANCER DOING THIS TO US? AND NOT AN EQUAL TO TALK TO ANYWHERE?!

GR-ASH

IS EVERYTHING ALL RIGHT, SIR? ARE YOU HURT?

NO, I'M FINE! LEAVE ME!

ACK!

WE HAVE MANAGED TO *HALT* THE RECONSTRUCTION OF THE SAND CASTLE. *DEAN PLUMB* HAS BEEN UNABLE TO--

IT'S NOT ENOUGH TO *STALL* THEM! MAKE SURE *PLUMB* GETS BLAMED FOR IT! GET HIM *HATED* THROUGHOUT *MON DOMANI!*

UM, YES, SIR. I'LL DO MY BEST, SIR.

MO ON YATTA

YES, SIR! OUR *AUTHORITY*...

...IS NEARLY *RESTORED!*

OUR TEAMS ARE DEALING WITH THE LAST POCKETS OF *RESISTANCE* AS WE SPEAK.

KRAK

AND THE PRINCE?

ERM, UNFORTUNATELY, THE *BOMBING* WAS... UNSUCCESSFUL....

WHAT?!

149

I REMEMBER
LEAVING MY
*PRINCE FELID
BODY.*

I REMEMBER
NOW.

I REMEMBER IT ALL.

WE'LL NAME HIM... *AN TZU.*

* SEE 5W2: *THE COBALT PRINCE*

156

AND YOUR ONLY TICKET HOME IS *US LIGHTING ALL FIVE BEACONS....*

WE HAVEN'T EVEN FOUND THE *AMBER ANTHEM,* NEVER MIND *TEN THOUSAND* PEOPLE TO SING IT!

OH, *AN TZU,* WHAT ARE WE GOING TO DO?

THERE MUST BE A WAY OF *REVERSING* THAT HOURGLASS FOR A BIT...BUYING MORE TIME....

HOW?

I DON'T KNOW, BUT...I'M A *FELID GOD.* THERE MUST BE A WAY! WHY WOULD I SET AN HOURGLASS ANYWAY? IT DOESN'T MAKE SENSE!

IT ONLY MAKES SENSE IF...

IF WHAT?

IF YOU **KNEW** THE FIVE WORLDS ARE **ALSO** RUNNING OUT OF TIME, AND YOU WERE DESPERATE TO SAVE THEM.

RISKING YOUR LIFE FOR ALL OF US.

WE WON'T LET YOU DOWN, **AN TZU.** WE'RE GOING TO DO THIS. TOGETHER.

YES, **TOGETHER.** WE'RE GOING TO SAVE **YOU** TOO!

MESSAGE FOR OONA LEE! YOU'LL NEVER BELIEVE WHO IT'S FROM!

WHAT? YOU OPENED IT?

IT'S FROM CASCADELLE!

OONA!

YOU CAME BACK FOR ME!

HOW CAN WE BE SURE SHE MADE IT?

WE'LL KNOW WHEN SHE *PORTALS* BACK TO THE INN WITH *O'ZIRG*.

PUT ME THROUGH TO *MR. MOON* RIGHT AWAY. HE'LL WANT TO HEAR THIS.

WHAT'S TAKING THEM SO LONG, *RAM SAM SAM?*

DON'T YOU THINK *OONA* SHOULD BE BACK ALREADY?

I TOLD THEM I'D BE ABLE TO HELP, BUT THEY WERE ALL, "NO, YOU NEED TO STAY SAFE."

THEY THINK I'M STILL JUST SOME STREET KID FROM *MON DOMANI.*

BUT YOU KNOW I'M *NOT,* RIGHT?

RRm Sm?

I'M *PRINCE FELID.* IT'S TIME I ACTED LIKE IT.

THE MAIN PRISON? IT'S THAT WAY, THEN BEAR LEFT AT THE STATUE.

YOU CAN'T ESCAPE! SURRENDER!

166

167

WHAT HAPPENED? HOW DID I GET HERE?

HEY, KID, YOU HURT?

EXCUSE ME, I KNOW HIM.

AN TZU, WHAT HAPPENED? ARE YOU INJURED?

I'M OKAY. HE BACKED OFF! I DON'T KNOW *WHY*. HE COULD'VE *KILLED* ME THEN AND THERE.

Chapter 13
AT CASCADELLE'S

UM, HELLO?

MISS CASCADELLE? I'M--

OONA! I'M SO GLAD TO FINALLY MEET YOU! THE REAL *"TOKI GIRL FROM MON DOMANI"*!

THANK YOU FOR INVITING US. IT'S AN HONOR--

NONSENSE! THE HONOR'S ALL MINE. YOU KIDS ARE *AMAZING*!

JAX AMBOY! AN TZU! LET ME HUG YOU TOO.

COME, HAVE SOME TEA.

AND LET'S TALK ABOUT THIS *AMBER ANTHEM*.

A LITTLE HARD TO UNDERSTAND, ISN'T IT?

I THINK YOU'RE SUPPOSED TO *FEEL* IT, EVEN IF YOU DON'T *UNDERSTAND* ALL THE WORDS.

BUT WHAT DO YOU THINK IT'S SAYING?

WELL, ITS OTHER TITLE IS *"ALL THE LIVING."* I THINK IT MEANS WE'RE ALL IN THIS TOGETHER, AND ALL THE *SAME* IN WHAT REALLY MATTERS.

OKAY...

AND *ALL* ARE NEEDED TO SING THE AMBER ANTHEM.

"ALL" MEANING THOSE TEN THOUSAND VOICES?

YES, BUT THINGS GET A BIT *TRICKY* AT THIS POINT....

"TRICKY"?

I THOUGHT THINGS GOT *TRICKY* THE MOMENT WE LANDED HERE!

WELL, IT SAYS HERE **THE TEN THOUSAND VOICES** HAVE TO REPRESENT THE **"FIVE RACES."**

FIVE RACES?!

WAIT, WE NEED NOT JUST **TEN THOUSAND** PEOPLE BUT ALSO **FIVE RACES** TO LIGHT THIS BEACON?!

I HAVEN'T BEEN ABLE TO FIGURE OUT **WHAT** THE FIVE RACES ARE.

DOES IT MEAN **BLUE-SKINNED TOKI** LIKE YOU AND ME--ONE RACE--AND **SALASSI** PEOPLE AS ANOTHER RACE...?

NO, THIS HERE SUGGESTS ALL FLESHY HUMANS ARE **ONE RACE.**

THERE'S THE **PLANT PEOPLE,** LIKE **ASH, SYCAMORE,** AND **CEDAR** OVER THERE. THAT'S **TWO.**

AND THE **KYOJIN!** THAT MAKES **THREE.**

EXACTLY--THE **KYOJIN,** LIKE **URUM** OVER HERE.

AFTER THAT, IT'S A BLANK. SOME ARCHIVES MENTION LUMINOUS BEINGS CALLED THE *SALASSI DEVOTI*...

BUT I HONESTLY THINK THAT'S A *LEGEND*--

NOT A LEGEND.

-SHI ING-

JOINED YOU?

I MET THEM.
ON MY FIRST VISIT
TO *SALASSANDRA.*
ONE OF THEM
JOINED ME.

YES, *THAT'S RIGHT!*
NOW *WHAT* COULD BE
THE *FIFTH*--?

I CAN
REPRESENT
THE *SALASSI
DEVOTI.*

RRM

LET'S SEE...
THAT LITTLE SYMBOL
LOOKS LIKE... WHAT
DOES IT LOOK
LIKE...?

EXCUSE ME,
RAM SAM SAM,
YOU'RE IN THE WAY.

179

WE NEED TO DO THIS AT THE **BEACON!**

CAN WE **SNEAK THERE** WITHOUT BEING SPOTTED?

NO, USE A **PORTAL!**

WAIT, NO... I THINK WE NEED TO GO DOWN THE MAIN AVENUE. IN **BROAD DAYLIGHT!**

I BELIEVE... I BELIEVE WE SHOULD!

BUT, OONA, YOU CAN'T BE OUT IN THE OPEN! THAT **KILLER ANDROID...**

IT'S THE ONLY WAY TO GATHER THE **CROWD** WE NEED, **JAX.** I KNOW YOU'LL KEEP ME SAFE.

SO...
FRIENDS?

I'LL THINK
ABOUT IT.

POFF

POFF

LITTLE **RAM SAM SAM** IS PART OF A HUGE ENTITY!

YOU NEED TO REJOIN IT. I UNDERSTAND.

THANK YOU, **RAM SAM SAM.** GO BE WHAT YOU ARE.

TEN THOUSAND VOICES!!

I LOVE YOU, RAM SAM SAM.

AN TZU...?

Chapter 15
SEAWEED SALAD

WE'LL NEED TO FILE PAPERWORK AND RECLAIM THE *FLITORI.* IT MAY TAKE TIME.

YOU MUST GO AHEAD. LIGHT THE LAST BEACON!

OONA, YOU NEED TO MAKE A PORTAL...TO *GRIMBO-E!*

THAT'S *POSSIBLE,* RIGHT?

A PORTAL TO *ANOTHER WORLD*...I'LL NEED ALL OF YOU.

WAIT... I'VE NEVER BEEN TO *GRIMBO-E!* HOW DO I TUNE IN TO IT?

WE STILL HAVE SOME *SEAWEED SALAD* FROM *MINTZ!*

YOU DO?!

THAT MIGHT WORK!

MNCH MNCH

THAT'S ON THE MAIN *LICHEN ISLAND!* IT'S *GRIMBO-E,* ALL RIGHT.

CAN I EAT THE REST OF THAT?

219

AN TZU?

UH...NOT HUNGRY ANYMORE.

GAH!

TO BE CONCLUDED IN 5W5: *THE EMERALD GATE*

To my 5W teammates, one thousand pages on —MS

To Shudan —AS

To my beloved felids, Beepboop and Yeti —XB

To those who fight for what they believe in —MR

To Mom —BS

ACKNOWLEDGMENTS

Thank you, champions Tanya McKinnon, Fauzia Burke, and Kane Lee

Our exquisite Random House team:
Chelsea Eberly, Michelle Nagler, Elizabeth Tardiff, Diane Landolf, Kelly McGauley,
Joshua Redlich, Adrienne Waintraub, Janine Perez, Alison Kolani,
Jen Jie Li, Jocelyn Lange, Lauren Morgan, Mallory Loehr, Barbara Marcus

+ Special thanks for added help, friendship, and magic:
Edward & Marie-Claire, Siena, Clio & Julien, Sonia, Felix & Elia, Shudan,
Julie Sandfort, Cynthia Cheng, Sasha Marciano

And Bryan Konietzko, Kazu Kibuishi, Lisa Yee, Noelle Stevenson,
Gene Luen Yang, Vera Brosgol, George O'Connor, Sara Varon, Ben Hatke

And thank you, dear fans young and old, for inviting others into the Five Worlds,
and thank you friends and allies among booksellers, librarians,
teachers, bloggers, and reviewers. We love to hear from you.

MARK SIEGEL has written and illustrated several award-winning picture books and graphic novels. He is also the editorial and creative director of First Second Books. He lives with his family in New York. Discover more at marksiegelbooks.com.

ALEXIS SIEGEL is a writer and translator based in Switzerland. He has translated a number of bestselling graphic novels, including Joann Sfar's *The Rabbi's Cat* and Pénélope Bagieu's *Exquisite Corpse* (both into English), and Gene Luen Yang's *American Born Chinese* (into French).

XANTHE BOUMA is an illustrator, comics artist, and colorist for animation and books. Based in Southern California, Xanthe enjoys soaking up the beachside sun.

MATT ROCKEFELLER is an illustrator and comics artist who grew up in Tucson, Arizona, and draws inspiration from its dramatic landscapes. His work has appeared in a variety of formats, including animation, book covers, and picture books such as *Pop!* and *Poesy the Monster Slayer*. He lives in Portland, Oregon, with his partner and a small dog that may or may not be a fox.

BOYA SUN loves to draw colorful comics about youth and adventure and is the creator of the graphic novel *Chasma Knights*. Originally from China, Boya has traveled from Canada to the United States and now lives in Los Angeles.

A Sneak Peek at the Making of 5W4

SUPERNOVAS, ATOMS, SANDCASTLES,
GREENHOUSES, GAZEBOS, LATTICES,

DOORWAYS
ARE OFTEN PORTALS
TO OTHER SOMETHINGS

1
buzzed/long side

2
high bob cut

3
pixie

4
soft/round

5
buzzed/braid

lavender

ash

olive

mint

blue

BUSINESS URMUTH

Discover more online!

jo_rioux

eclipse_orion

masqueradesage.art

herro_cubes

eleoradraws

beside_wais

gay_as_a_pineapple

STAY TUNED
FOR CONTESTS
AND SPECIAL EVENTS
ON A PLANET NEAR YOU!

Where will the epic adventure end?
Find out in

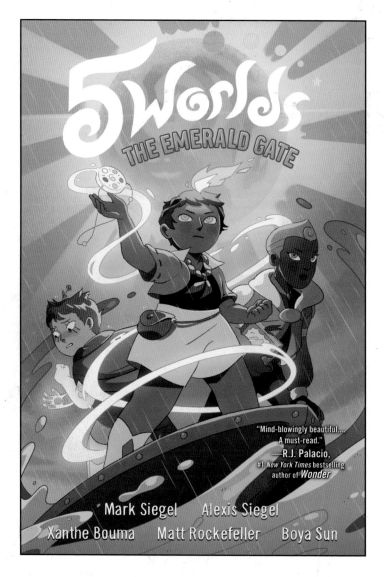

5W5:
THE EMERALD GATE